AMANDA PIG
AND THE
REALLY HOT DAY

by Jean Van Leeuwen
pictures by Ann Schweninger

DIAL BOOKS FOR YOUNG READERS
New York

For Elizabeth,
with fond memories of lemonade stands
—J. V. L.

For Mom with love
—A. S.

Published by Dial Books for Young Readers
A division of Penguin Young Readers Group
345 Hudson Street
New York, New York 10014
Text copyright © 2005 by Jean Van Leeuwen
Pictures copyright © 2005 by Ann Schweninger
All rights reserved
Designed by Jasmin Rubero
Manufactured in China on acid-free paper
The Dial Easy-to-Read logo is a registered trademark of
Dial Books for Young Readers,
a division of Penguin Young Readers Group ® TM 1,162,718.

1   3   5   7   9   10   8   6   4   2

Library of Congress Cataloging-in-Publication Data
Van Leeuwen, Jean.
Amanda Pig and the really hot day /
by Jean Van Leeuwen ; pictures by Ann Schweninger.
p.   cm.
"Dial Easy-to-Read."
Summary: Amanda Pig and her family and friends try
to find different ways to beat the heat.
ISBN 0-8037-2887-5
[1. Pigs—Fiction. 2. Heat—Fiction. 3. Family life—Fiction.]
I. Schweninger, Ann, ill. II. Title.
PZ7.V275Amk 2005   [E]—dc21   2003010401

The full-color artwork was prepared using carbon pencil,
colored pencils, and watercolor washes.

Reading Level 1.8

CONTENTS

THE HOTTEST DAY

"I was never so hot in my whole life,"

said Amanda.

"My nose is hot. My knees are hot.

Even my hair ribbons are hot.

"Can we go swimming?"

"Not today," said Mother.

"Maybe a glass of water would help."

Amanda drank a glass of water.

"I'm still hot," she said.

"Maybe some lemonade would help."

"Okay," said Mother.

Amanda drank a glass of lemonade.

"Oops!" she said.

She spilled a little on her shorts.

"Now I'm hot and sticky," she said.

"Maybe something very cold would help.

Can I have an ice pop?"

"All right," said Mother.

Amanda picked grape, her favorite.

"Uh-oh," she said.

The ice pop was melting faster

than she could eat it.

It dripped down her chin.

It dripped down her elbows.

It dripped all over her shirt.

"Now I'm hot and sticky and drippy!"

she cried.

Mother cleaned her up.

"Why don't you go outside

and see what Father is doing?" she said.

It was even hotter outside

with the sun shining down.

Father was in the garden.

"Why are you wearing that funny hat?"

asked Amanda.

"To keep my head cool," said Father.

"But I can't keep the garden cool.

Look at our tomatoes.

Look at our string beans.

Look at our squash and cucumbers."

"They are all droopy," said Amanda.

"Just like me. I am hot

and sticky and drippy and droopy."

"I have an idea," said Father.

"Close your eyes

and I will give you a hot-day surprise."

"That's a poem!" said Amanda.

Amanda stood next to the cucumbers.

She closed her eyes.

She could feel the sun burning down.

She was getting hotter and hotter.

Any minute she would melt.

"Father!" she called. "Where are you?"

"Right here," said Father.

"Are you ready?"

"Yes," said Amanda.

All of a sudden it was raining.

Cool, wet, wonderful rain!

How could that be?

"You can open your eyes now," said Father.

"You watered me," said Amanda.

"Yes," said Father.

"Now I'm not hot and sticky

and drippy and droopy," said Amanda.

"I am cool."

"Me too," said Father.

OLIVER'S FORT

Oliver and his friends

were building a fort in the backyard.

"Can I help?" asked Amanda.

"No," said Oliver.

"No girls allowed," said Albert.

"Go away," said James.

Amanda went away. But not too far.

She listened.

"We need some rope," said Albert.

"You can use my jump rope,"

said Amanda.

"We told you to go away," said Oliver.

"We told you no girls allowed,"

said Albert.

"And no little kids either," said James.

"I'm not a little kid," said Amanda.

She went away. But not too far.

She watched.

"Are you spying, Amanda?" called Oliver.

"You know what we do to spies,"

said Albert.

"Specially little kid girl spies," said James.

Amanda went inside.

"Oliver is mean," she said.

"He won't let me help build his fort."

"Oliver is building a fort?" said Mother.

"On such a hot day? How silly.

Today is a day to sit in the shade

and do nothing.

Maybe Lollipop would like to come over."

Amanda called Lollipop.

"It's too hot to play," said Lollipop.

"We won't play," said Amanda.

"We will sit in the shade and do nothing."

Amanda and Lollipop sat in the shade

of the apple tree and did nothing at all.

After a while they had some lemonade.

"It's a tea party," said Lollipop.

Then they did nothing some more.

"This is fun," said Lollipop.

"And cool," said Amanda.

"I'm so hot!" said Oliver.

"Building a fort is hard work."

"We need a drink," said Albert.

"Quick," said James,

"give us some lemonade!"

"You can't have our lemonade,"

said Amanda.

"Please?" said Oliver.

"No," said Lollipop.

"No boys allowed under the apple tree,"

said Amanda. "And no big kids."

"You're mean," said Oliver.

"I know," said Amanda.

"But you were mean first."

"Really really mean," said Lollipop.

"Maybe," said Amanda,

"we might give you some

if you let us see your fort."

Oliver looked at Albert.

Albert looked at James.

"I'm so thirsty," said James,

"I could drink a whole ocean."

"Okay," said Oliver.

"You can come see our fort,

but you can't help build it."

"Who wants to help build it?"

said Lollipop. "It's too hot."

So Amanda and Lollipop

and Oliver and Albert and James

all had lemonade in Oliver's fort.

THE LEMONADE STAND

"Everyone wants lemonade

on such a hot day," said Amanda.

"Let's have a lemonade stand."

"Yes!" said Lollipop.

So they took Amanda's little table

and a pitcher of lemonade

and sat beside the road.

"I bet we'll sell lots and lots

of lemonade," said Amanda.

"And make lots and lots

of money," said Lollipop.

"I could buy Tracy

the Talking, Walking Doll."

"I could buy a new purple bike,"
said Amanda.

They waited for everyone to come
and buy lemonade.

But no one came.

"Maybe it's too hot," said Amanda.

"Maybe everyone is sitting in the shade doing nothing."

"I'm too hot," said Lollipop.

"I need a drink."

They both had a drink of lemonade.

They waited some more.

"Hello, Amanda! Isn't this a hot day?"

It was Mrs. Clara Pig from next door.

"Would you like to buy some lemonade?"

asked Amanda and Lollipop.

"Maybe later," said Mrs. Clara Pig.

"Now I have to put away my groceries."

Amanda and Lollipop

had another drink of lemonade.

They waited some more.

"Oh boy, lemonade! Let me at it!"

It was William and Sam and Spencer

from their class at school.

"You have to pay us," said Lollipop.

"But we don't have any money,"

said William.

"Sorry," said Amanda.

The boys rode away.

"Business is bad," said Amanda.

"Now I'll never get my new purple bike."

They had some more lemonade.

"Hi, sweetie! Hi, Amanda!"

It was Lollipop's mother

and her baby sister, Lulu.

"Two cups of lemonade, please," she said.

Amanda picked up the pitcher.

"Uh-oh," she said.

"We drank it all."

"No one came," said Lollipop.

"And we got thirsty."

"Lem-ade!" cried Lulu. "Want lem-ade!"

"I'll have some too," said Mrs. Clara Pig.

"We've got money now,"

said William and Sam and Spencer.

"Give us three cups."

"It's all gone," said Amanda.

"Lem-ade! Lem-ade! Lem-ade!"

wailed Lulu, jumping up and down.

"Coming right up."

It was Mother. She was carrying

a new pitcher of lemonade

and a plate of cookies.

"Thank you!" said Amanda.

They poured lemonade for everyone.

"That was hard work," said Lollipop.

"We didn't make lots and lots

of money," said Amanda. "But it was fun."

"Would you girls like a drink?"

asked Mother.

"No," said Amanda and Lollipop.

"No more lemonade."

THE HOTTEST NIGHT

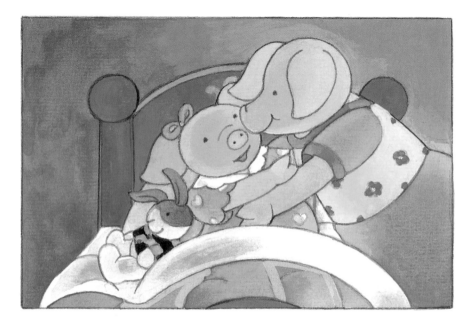

"Good night, Amanda," said Mother.

"Good night," said Amanda.

She tried to go to sleep.

But her pajamas were too hot.

Her quilt was too hot.

Hugging Sallie Rabbit was too hot.

"Mother!" she called.

"What is it?" asked Mother.

"It's too hot to sleep," said Amanda.

"I think you are right," said Mother.

"Why don't we sit outside

for a little while?

Maybe we will feel a cool breeze."

Mother and Amanda sat in the grass.

"I don't feel a cool breeze," said Amanda.

"No," said Mother. "Not yet."

"What are you doing outside?"
asked Oliver.

"It's too hot to sleep," said Amanda.

"We are waiting for a cool breeze."

"I can't sleep either," said Oliver.

"I'm as hot as a fried egg.

I'm as hot as toast.

I'm as hot as oatmeal."

"Move over," said Amanda.

"You're making me hotter."

"Oh, there you are," said Father.

"I've been looking everywhere."

"We are waiting for a cool breeze,"

said Oliver.

"But there is no breeze at all.

I'm as hot as spaghetti in a pot."

42

"I'm as hot as a meatball," said Amanda.

"Let's not think about it," said Father.

"Let's look at the stars instead."

"Can you count them?" asked Mother.

Amanda tried.

"Twenty-two, twenty-three," she said.

"I give up."

"A million billion," said Oliver.

"I'm still hot. As hot as hot chocolate."

"Let me tell you a story," said Father.

"Once upon a time

there was a polar bear.

His name was Snowball

and he lived at the North Pole,

where it is always cold."

"Did he have a sister?" asked Amanda.

"Yes, he did," said Father.

"Her name was Ice Pop."

"That's silly," said Amanda.

"Every day Snowball and Ice Pop

played in the snow," said Father.

"They went sledding down ice hills

and skating on ice ponds.

They made snow bears and snow forts."

"And snow angels," said Amanda.

"And do you know what they ate for breakfast, lunch, and dinner?" asked Father.

"Ice cream?" said Oliver.

"That's right," said Father.

"And then their mother tucked them in and Snowball and Ice Pop went to sleep in their nice, cool ice house."

"That was a nice, cool story,"

said Amanda.

"Oh my," said Mother. "I think I feel it.

A cool breeze."

"I feel it too," said Father.

"Hooray!" said Oliver.

"I'm as cool as a pool."

"Finally," said Amanda.